# A Present for Mrs. Kazinski

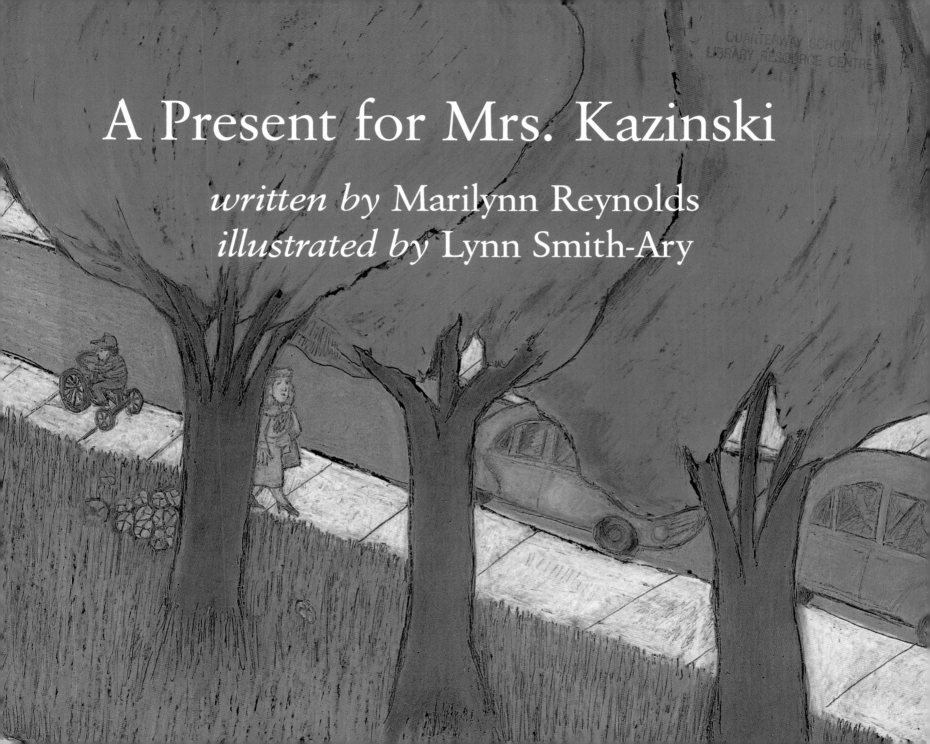

# A Present for Mrs. Kazinski

*written by* Marilynn Reynolds
*illustrated by* Lynn Smith-Ary

High up in the attic of an old house on Grant Street, Mrs. Kazinski sat at the window and looked out over the neighborhood. She sat there all day long and every day.

Frank lived downstairs in the old house, and when he played outside, he remembered to look up and wave. Mrs. Kazinski was the oldest person Frank knew. Her face was covered with wrinkles because she smiled a lot, and she smelled good, like lavender sachets and old books.

The rickety house on Grant Street was bursting at its seams.

Frank and his mother rented the kitchen and back bedrooms. Frank's mother was a cook. She worked in a fish-and-chip shop on Commercial Drive, and she made the best deep-fried cod and french fries in the city.

Rose lived in the front bedroom.

She was a waitress with lots of yellow hair. She cooked her dinners on a hotplate, and she let Frank watch her curl her eyelashes with a long, shiny, metal eyelash curler.

Captain Pittaway, a military man straight as a ramrod, lived on the second floor. Frank liked to watch him wax his moustaches. They were very long, very curly moustaches, and Captain Pittaway was extremely proud of them.

A fat and happy cat lived under the front porch. At night she hunted for mice in the tall weeds in the yard. She was nobody's cat — she belonged to herself.

Mrs. Kazinski and Frank were best friends, and he often climbed the dark attic steps to visit her. They drank cups of tea with lots of milk and sugar, and Mrs. Kazinski showed him her photograph album with pictures of herself when she was a little girl. Every Saturday afternoon she got all dressed up and took Frank to the movies on Commercial Drive. Frank liked her best of all the people in the house, next to his mother.

"I'm going to have a birthday on Sunday," Mrs. Kazinski told him one day. "I'm going to be eighty years old, and I'm going to bake an apple strudel and cover it with candles and have a birthday party for myself. Everybody in the house will be invited."

"Mrs. Kazinski is going to have a birthday on Sunday," Frank told his mother after work. "She's going to be eighty years old."

"That's pretty old," said Mother.

"I want to get her a special birthday present," Frank said. "A birthday present for someone who's very, very old." He frowned. "It has to be the best present in the world."

Mother said, "Well, everybody likes food. Why don't you get her some honey doughnuts, or a jar of strawberry jam, or a package of mints? What about a box of sugar cookies or shortbread or gingersnaps?"

"What'll I get Mrs. Kazinski for her birthday?" he asked Rose. "It has to be the best present in the world."

"Have you thought about perfume?" she said. "That's my favorite. Or Mrs. Kazinski would like bath salts or face powder or body lotion or cleansing cream or mascara." Rose smiled at Frank. "I know she can use lipstick and rouge in a nice shade of pink." Rose fluffed her hair. "All women want to smell good and look pretty."

Captain Pittaway had another idea.

"The best present in the world?" said the captain, sniffing the flowers in the park across the street. "Flowers, my boy, flowers are the answer. Get her a bouquet of daisies or petunias or snapdragons . . . or maybe foxgloves, bachelor's buttons, daffodils, baby's breath, pansies . . . or delphiniums, geraniums, nasturtiums, pelargoniums or alliums." Captain Pittaway caught his breath. "Women love flowers."

Frank looked in the windows of the five-and-dime and the hardware store on Commercial Drive. The stores were full of things, but Mrs. Kazinski already had cups and saucers, glittery earrings, china ornaments, lace doilies, plastic flowers and fancy pens in leather boxes.

My present has to be better than anything I could buy in a store, Frank thought.

Frank went home and drew a big picture for Mrs. Kazinski, but he didn't think it was good enough for a birthday present. He found a pine cone in the yard and tried to paint it with his watercolors, but it didn't turn out very well.

On the morning of the birthday, Frank collected some shiny stones he thought Mrs. Kazinski would like. And he found some ferns with long, curving stems. But he wasn't happy.

I want it to be the best present in the world, he thought.

Then Frank saw a kitten in the grass. The small creature came up and touched his fingers with its cold little nose. Frank petted it. He thought about Mrs. Kazinski, and he had an idea.

"Do you think your kitten's big enough to leave you?" he asked the mother cat. The mother cat purred and rubbed against Frank's leg.

"You're going to be a birthday present," Frank said to the kitten as he carried it back to the house. "The best present in the world."

Frank liked the kitten. He liked the way it lapped up the milk he poured into a saucer. And when it yawned, Frank liked its pink tongue and its sharp little teeth. He liked the way it chased a piece of yarn and rolled around on the floor. He liked the kitten so much, he didn't want to give it away.

He thought about his friend, Mrs. Kazinski, living all by herself, watching other people from her window day after day.

Frank played with the kitten all afternoon. The more they played, the sadder he felt. When evening came, Frank put the kitten in a box and began to wrap it up.

The kitten wouldn't stay in the box, so Frank put a bow around its neck, picked it up and started upstairs to Mrs. Kazinski's birthday party. He climbed very, very slowly. The stairway to the attic had never seemed so steep, and his feet felt heavier with each step.

"Why, Frank!" Mrs. Kazinski said when she opened the door. "You're the first person here." She looked down at his hands. "And you've brought me a kitten for my birthday!"

Mrs. Kazinski leaned over stiffly and took the kitten. "I haven't had a kitten since I was a girl," she said.

Mrs. Kazinski sat down in her armchair and stroked the kitten with her worn hands. "And it's such a beautiful little thing. I know we're going to be great friends."

Mrs. Kazinski looked at Frank's woeful face. She pulled him to her side. "Are you sure you want to give me the kitten?" she asked.

Frank nodded. "You're my friend," he said bravely. "I wanted to give you the best present in the world."

Mrs. Kazinski raised his chin. "You couldn't have given me a nicer present," she said. "Now I have a pet to live with me and keep me company. But I want you to promise that you'll come to visit the kitten every day."

Mrs. Kazinski's eyes smiled out at Frank from a thousand wrinkles, and suddenly he felt very, very pleased.

Just then there was a knock at the door, and Captain Pittaway strode in with a flower in his lapel and a bouquet in his hand. "Happy birthday, dear lady," he said with a bow.

Rose rushed in from her shift at the café with a bottle of bright red nail polish for Mrs. Kazinski. And last of all, Frank's mother ran breathlessly up the stairs, carrying hot fish and chips she'd just cooked in the shop. They were wrapped in newspaper and smelled deliciously of salt and vinegar.

Everyone sat down at Mrs. Kazinski's table and ate the fish and chips before they got cold.

Rose lit the candles on the strudel until it blazed like a small forest fire. And everyone sang "Happy Birthday."

Mrs. Kazinski stood up. "My dear friends," she said, "thank you for your lovely gifts." She looked around the table at each smiling face. "I've had eighty birthdays in my lifetime, but this is the happiest one of all."

Mrs. Kazinski blew out the candles and cut the strudel into five very, very big pieces.

It was the best strudel in the world.

When I was a child, I lived in many different houses
in many parts of the country. In each and every one
of them, an elderly lady lived up in the attic, in a suite
in the basement, in the house next door or in the
apartment down the street. These women became
my friends, and I want to dedicate this book to
their memory: to Mrs. Wright, Mrs. Wilson,
Mrs. Cummings, Mrs. Struthers, Miss Lettice Pearson,
Miss Cuthbertson and dear Bessie Wozencroft.

M.R.

To my parents, Dr. and Mrs. Alexander B. Smith,
and my husband, Zander Ary.

L.S-A.

Text copyright © 2001 Marilynn Reynolds
Illustration copyright © 2001 Lynn Smith-Ary

Canadian Cataloguing in Publication Data
Reynolds, Marilynn, 1940-
A present for Mrs. Kazinski

ISBN 1-55143-196-3 (bound) — ISBN 1-55143-198-X (pbk.)

I. Smith-Ary, Lynn, 1942-   II. Title.
PS8585.E973P73 2001    jC813'.54    C00-911355-X
PZ7.R33732Pr 2001

Library of Congress Catalog Card Number: 00-110529

Orca Book Publishers gratefully acknowledges the support of
our publishing programs provided by the following agencies:
the Department of Canadian Heritage, The Canada Council
for the Arts, and the British Columbia Arts Council.

Design by Christine Toller
Printed and bound in Hong Kong

IN CANADA:
Orca Book Publishers
PO Box 5626, Station B
Victoria, BC  Canada
V8R 6S4

IN THE UNITED STATES:
Orca Book Publishers
PO Box 468
Custer, WA  USA
98240-0468

03  02  01  •  5  4  3  2  1